Mrs. Davis felt peculiar as she took her morning bath.
"I feel like I'm being watched,"
she said to herself.
And she *was* being watched…

...by Shirley Rat, the nosiest person in town.

"I see you're using lilac bubble bath," said Shirley.

"I personally prefer rose."

Mrs. Davis pulled down the shade.

NOSEY MRS. RAT

JEFFREY ALLEN · JAMES MARSHALL

PUFFIN BOOKS

For Marilyn and Bill Welch

PUFFIN BOOKS
A Division of Penguin Books USA Inc.
375 Hudson Street, New York, New York 10014
Harmondsworth, Middlesex, England (Distribution & Warehouse)
Penguin Books Australia Ltd, Ringwood, Victoria, Australia
Penguin Books Canada Limited, 2801 John Street, Markham, Ontario, Canada L3R 1B4
Penguin Books (N.Z.) Ltd, 182–190 Wairau Road, Auckland 10, New Zealand
First published by Viking Penguin Inc., 1985
Published in Picture Puffins 1987
Reprinted 1987
Text copyright © Jeffrey Allen, 1985
Illustrations copyright © James Marshall, 1985
All rights reserved

Set in Times Roman.

LIBRARY OF CONGRESS CATALOGING IN PUBLICATION DATA
Allen, Jeffrey.   Nosey Mrs. Rat.
Reprint. Originally published: New York, N.Y.:
Viking Kestrel, 1985.
Summary: Mrs. Rat makes a career out of spying on her
neighbors, but the tables are unexpectedly turned on her.
[1. Rats—Fiction.   2. Curiosity—Fiction]
I. Marshall, James, 1942–   , ill.   II. Title.
[PZ7.A4272No 1987]   [E]   86-25462   ISBN 0-14-050665-9

"I love to know what's going on," said Shirley.
"I don't get paid for it—
it's my hobby."
And Shirley's hobby kept her very busy.

Reading other people's mail took half the morning.
"You learn *such* interesting things,"
said Shirley.

Listening in on private telephone conversations,
Shirley sometimes forgot to fix lunch for her kids.
"First things first," said Shirley.

In the afternoon Shirley did lots of snoopy things—
like poking around in other people's shopping carts.
"Can you really afford this expensive brand?"
she said to Mrs. Butler.

And at night, while people were watching television, Shirley Rat was watching *them*.

"There's a more amusing program on Channel Five," said Shirley.

Sometimes Shirley wore a disguise.

"I can find out more if people don't recognize me,"
she said.

"There's that nosey Shirley Rat,"
whispered one of her neighbors.

Most folks had gotten used to Shirley's little ways.

"There's one in every town," they said.

But not *everyone* was so understanding.

"I hate that Mrs. Rat," said Brewster Blackstone,
who lived next door. "She makes my life *miserable.*"
Brewster Blackstone couldn't get away with a thing.
"Shouldn't you boys be in school?" said Shirley,
just when Brewster and his gang thought they were safe.

"I'm so sorry to hear Brewster flunked history,"
said Shirley to Mr. Blackstone.
"He *did?*" said Brewster's dad.
"That's the first *I've* heard of it."

Brewster Blackstone was grounded for a whole week.

And he had plenty of time to think.

"This calls for a creative solution,"

said Brewster.

One afternoon, while Shirley Rat was engaged in her
favorite activity, something attracted her attention.
"Hmm," said Shirley.

The postman had just delivered
a large and interesting package to Brewster.
"Ooh, ooh," said Shirley. "I wonder what's inside."

"Brewster, dear," said Shirley in her sweetest voice,
"what is in that large and interesting package
the postman just delivered?"
"None of your beeswax," said Brewster.

And he hung up.

"How rude," said Shirley.

"I'll find out what's in that package
if it's the last thing I do!"

Using her special sticky shoes,
Shirley scaled the Blackstones' house
to get a look in Brewster's window.
But Brewster had pulled down the shade.

Next Shirley sifted through the Blackstones' garbage.
"You never know what clues you'll find," she said.
But the Blackstones' garbage gave Shirley no clues.

Shirley tried to disguise herself
to get inside Brewster's room.
"I'm the Roach Patrol," said Shirley.
"I know who you are," said Mrs. Blackstone.

At home, Shirley had trouble concentrating.
"That package is really none of your business,"
said her husband.
But he wasn't heard.

Shirley went to the park to sit and think.

Suddenly she spotted a small envelope marked
CONFIDENTIAL—DO NOT OPEN.

"Oh goody," said Shirley.

The card read: SNEAK PREVIEW—INVITATION ONLY
BREWSTER BLACKSTONE'S BACKYARD AT 8.
"I *love* sneak previews!" said Shirley.
At Brewster's Shirley took a front-row seat.

The film began.

"Oh my," said Shirley.

"There is nothing worse

than a nosey neighbor."

Suddenly, for everyone to see, there was Shirley Rat
up to her old tricks—snooping shamelessly.
The audience began to laugh out loud.
"What's so funny?" said Shirley.

And when the film showed Shirley trying
different ways to peek in Brewster's window,
someone called out, "That's our Nosey Mrs. Rat."
"Nosey?" said Shirley. *"Nosey?"*
Soon the audience was in hysterics.
They laughed so hard they fell out of their seats.
Shirley made a quick exit.
"I'm so humiliated!" she said.

At home Shirley went straight to bed.

"I'll never snoop again," she said.

"There, there," said her husband.

"Perhaps you can save snooping for special occasions."

"Oh, *no,*" said Shirley. "I'm finished with all that."

"Well, you have a nice rest, dear," said Mr. Rat.

And he gently closed the door.

"Hmmm," said Shirley.

"Well, perhaps for special occasions…"